Dear Parent:
Your child's love of reading starts here!

Every child learns to read in a different way and at his or her own speed. Some go back and forth between reading levels and read favorite books again and again. Others read through each level in order. You can help your young reader improve and become more confident by encouraging his or her own interests and abilities. From books your child reads with you to the first books he or she reads alone, there are I Can Read Books for every stage of reading:

SHARED READING
Basic language, word repetition, and whimsical illustrations, ideal for sharing with your emergent reader

BEGINNING READING
Short sentences, familiar words, and simple concepts for children eager to read on their own

READING WITH HELP
Engaging stories, longer sentences, and language play for developing readers

READING ALONE
Complex plots, challenging vocabulary, and high-interest topics for the independent reader

I Can Read Books have introduced children to the joy of reading since 1957. Featuring award-winning authors and illustrators and a fabulous cast of beloved characters, I Can Read Books set the standard for beginning readers.

A lifetime of discovery begins with the magical words "I Can Read!"

Visit www.icanread.com for information
on enriching your child's reading experience.

For Gab and Josh, who
always bring me joy
—K.S.L.

For Aria Rose
and our pal Hudson
—N.M.

Ty's Travels: All Aboard!
Text copyright © 2020 by Kelly Starling Lyons
Illustrations copyright © 2020 by Nina Mata

Library of Congress Control Number: 2019945991
ISBN 978-0-06-295112-0 (trade bdg.) — ISBN 978-0-06-295107-6 (pbk.)

Book design by Rachel Zegar
20 21 22 23 24 LSC 10 9 8 7 6 5 4 3 2 1
❖
First Edition

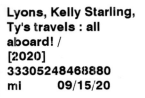

n Read!

TY'S TRAVELS

All Aboard!

By Kelly Starling Lyons   pictures by Nina Mata

HARPER
An Imprint of HarperCollinsPublishers

My name is Ty.

I love adventures.

I wish my family would play.
"Daddy, will you play
with me?"

"In a while, little man.
I'm cooking dinner."

I walk into the living room. "Momma, will you play with me?"

"Not right now, honey.
I'm folding clothes.
Want to help?"

I race upstairs
to my big brother's room.
"Corey, will you play
with me?"

"Sorry, Ty.

I'm doing homework."

I walk downstairs.

I spot an empty box.

I know just what to do.
Time for fun!

I climb inside.

The floor is the track.

The ceiling is the sky.

I drive the train.
I blow the whistle.
"Woo-woo!"

My train rumbles slowly.
Chugga-chugga-chugga-chugga.
Then it picks up steam.

Clickety-clack.

Clickety-clack.

Clickety-clack.

As I get to the first stop,
I spot someone waiting.
Daddy!

Daddy smiles and winks.
"All aboard!"

Our train rumbles slowly.

Chugga-chugga-chugga-chugga.

Then it picks up steam.

Clickety-clack.

Clickety-clack.

Clickety-clack.

Daddy blows the whistle.

"Woo-woo!"

We fly by farms and ponds.

At the next stop,
someone smiles and waves.
Momma!
"All aboard!"

Our train rumbles slowly.

Chugga-chugga-chugga-chugga.

Then it picks up steam.

Clickety-clack.

Clickety-clack.

Clickety-clack.

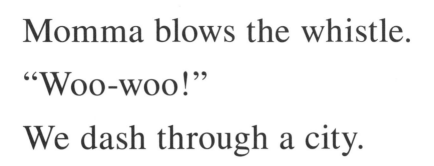

Momma blows the whistle.

"Woo-woo!"

We dash through a city.

At the next stop,
someone smiles
and points at me.
Corey!

"All aboard!"
Corey blows the whistle.
"Woo-woo!"

We chug across a bridge.
We zoom into a tunnel.
Momma and Daddy
cheer me on.

"Check out the view!"

Corey says.

We're on top of the world.

As we get to the next stop,
I smell something yummy.
I know just what to do.
"Last stop! Home."

Time for food!